A Whirlwind Vacation

For my super-duper parents—N.K.

For Barbara, world traveler—J&W

GROSSET & DUNLAP
Published by the Penguin Group
Penguin Group (USA) Inc., 375 Hudson Street, New York, New York 10014, U.S.A.
Penguin Group (Canada), 10 Alcorn Avenue, Toronto, Ontario, Canada M4V 3B2
(a division of Pearson Penguin Canada Inc.)
Penguin Books Ltd, 80 Strand, London WC2R 0RL, England
Penguin Ireland, 25 St Stephen's Green, Dublin 2, Ireland
(a division of Penguin Books Ltd)
Penguin Group (Australia), 250 Camberwell Road, Camberwell, Victoria 3124, Australia
(a division of Pearson Australia Group Pty Ltd)
Penguin Books India Pvt Ltd, 11 Community Centre,
Panchsheel Park, New Delhi - 110 017, India
Penguin Group (NZ), Cnr Airborne and Rosedale Roads, Albany, Auckland 1310,
New Zealand (a division of Pearson New Zealand Ltd)
Penguin Books (South Africa) (Pty) Ltd, 24 Sturdee Avenue,
Rosebank, Johannesburg 2196, South Africa

Penguin Books Ltd, Registered Offices:
80 Strand, London WC2R 0RL, England

Library of Congress Control Number: 2004029313

ISBN 0-448-43748-1   10 9 8 7 6 5 4 3 2 1

A Whirlwind Vacation

by Nancy Krulik • illustrated by John & Wendy

Grosset & Dunlap

Dear Grandma,

I am writing to you while I am on the airplane to London! Right now, Mom, Dad, and I are flying over the Atlantic Ocean. We will be in England in a few hours. Then our European vacation will really begin.

London, Paris, Madrid, Venice. I'm so excited, I haven't been able to sleep at all the entire trip! I promise to tell you all about it!

Wish you were here!

Love,
Katie

Gladys Stephens
New Mexico
USA

Dear Jeremy,

You would love it here in London. Everyone is a soccer fan! The funny thing is, the people in London call soccer "football."

This morning we visited a clock tower called Big Ben. It's got a thirteen-ton bell in it that really rings! I bet that alarm clock would get me out of bed!

Wish you were here!
Katie

Jeremy Fox
Cherrydale
USA

Chapter 1

"Oh, Mom, Dad, look at that beautiful building!" Katie Carew shouted as she rode through the streets of London, England, in a red double-decker bus. Katie thought the building they were riding past was the most amazing place she had ever seen. The huge red brick mansion was surrounded by big black and gold gates. There was a bright green lawn and beautiful gardens all around the building.

"That's Kensington Palace," Vicki, a woman with hair almost as red as Katie's, explained. Vicki was a tour guide. It was her job to tell the people in Katie's tour group all about the European cities they were visiting on their vacation.

"Is that where the Queen lives?" Katie asked her.

Vicki shook her head. "The Queen lives in Buckingham Palace. At least some of the time. She has several residences."

"Have you ever seen the Queen?" Katie asked.

Vicki nodded. "But only from a distance during a parade."

"I saw the president once," a girl with short, curly brown hair and big brown eyes piped up. She was sitting across the aisle from Katie and her parents. "When he came to Boston. Remember, Daddy?"

"I do, Annabelle," her father agreed. "But we only got a glimpse of his limousine."

The girl frowned. "Well, he was *in* the limo," she insisted.

"I think that's very exciting, Annabelle," Vicki said. She turned to Katie. "It looks like you girls are around the same age. I think you will be great mates on this journey."

Katie smiled at Annabelle. Even though Katie thought Annabelle seemed a little snobby, at least she was a kid. The rest of the group was all grown-ups.

Katie looked around the bus. In the front were the Penderbottoms, an older couple who liked art museums and shopping.

The Fishmans were on their honeymoon. They barely spoke to anyone else on the tour.

And they kissed *a lot*.

The Garcias and the McIntyres were two couples who went on vacation together every year. They were always taking pictures of one another in front of signs, statues, and buildings.

Miss Cornblau and Miss Framingham liked to sit in the back of the bus. They were teachers. Katie *really* didn't want to hang out with teachers. After all, she was on vacation.

So that left Annabelle. She was on this trip with her parents, the Bridgemans.

"So what do you think of London so far?" Katie asked Annabelle.

"I love it. Especially the accents. We don't talk like that in Boston," Annabelle answered.

"I think *everything* here is amazing," Katie said. "The buildings are so beautiful and so old."

"Well, I'm kind of used to old buildings. We have a lot of them in Boston," Annabelle boasted.

"Yes, but they're not *this* old," Mrs. Bridgeman said. "Remember, Annabelle, there was a London long before there was a Boston."

"Did you grow up in London?" Katie asked Vicki. She wanted to talk about England, not Boston.

The tour guide nodded. "I lived in London until I was eighteen. Then I moved around Europe a lot."

"You must speak quite a few languages," Katie's dad said.

"Oh, yes," Vicki replied. "I speak English, French, Spanish, and Italian. In fact, the only language I'll have trouble with on this trip is American."

Katie giggled. She'd only been in London for one day, but already she had found that English people used different words than Americans. They called the bathroom the "loo." They also called elevators "lifts." Sweaters were called "jumpers," and under-pants were called "knickers."

"I've never been happy staying in one place for very long," Vicki explained. "I like to go wherever the wind takes me."

Katie shuddered. That didn't sound good to her. Katie didn't like winds. Not at all.

That was because Katie knew the wind could take you places you didn't want to go. Or at least the *magic* wind could.

The magic wind was a wild tornado that blew just around Katie. It was so powerful that every time it came, it turned her into somebody else! Katie never knew when the wind would arrive. But when it did, her whole world was turned upside down . . . *switcheroo*!

Katie's adventures with the magic wind had started last year, when she was in third grade. She'd had a terrible day. First she'd lost the football game for her team. She'd gotten mud all over her favorite pants, and burped really loudly in front of the whole class. George Brennan started calling her Katie Kazoo, instead of Katie Carew. (Actually, now

Katie kind of liked that name!)

That night, Katie had wished she could be anyone other than herself. There must have been a shooting star overhead when she made that wish, because the very next day the magic wind came. It turned Katie into Speedy, the class hamster! Katie spent the whole morning going round and round on a hamster wheel!

The magic wind came back again and again after that. Sometimes it changed Katie into other kids—like her best friends, Jeremy and Suzanne. Other times it turned her into adults—like her school principal, Mr. Kane, or Louie, the man who owned the pizzeria in the Cherrydale Mall.

One time the wind had even turned her into her own cocker spaniel, Pepper. She'd chased after a squirrel and ruined her neighbor's garden. That was really bad since Katie's next-door neighbor was also her third-grade teacher, Mrs. Derkman.

Katie sure hoped that the magic wind hadn't followed her all the way across the Atlantic Ocean. She didn't want to be anyone else right now. She just wanted to stay Katie Kazoo and enjoy her super-duper European vacation!

Chapter 2

"Katie, do you remember when you were asking me about where the Queen lives?" Vicki said a while later.

Katie nodded.

"Well, we're going to go to Buckingham Palace next!" Vicki told her.

"Wow!" Katie exclaimed. "Do you think we'll see her? I wonder what she'll be wearing."

Vicki laughed. "I don't think we'll get to see the Queen today. But we will get a view of something *very* exciting. The Guard Mounting."

"What's that?" Annabelle asked her.

"Some people call it the changing of the guard," Vicki explained. "It's a ceremony in which the Queen's guards change places as they take turns watching over the palace."

"Are there always guards outside the palace?" Annabelle asked. "Even if the Queen isn't home?"

Vicki nodded. "Always. It's a very difficult job. The guards have to stand in one place for a very long time. They can't laugh or smile, no matter what happens."

"I'll bet my friend George could make the guards laugh," Katie told Vicki. "He's the funniest kid in the whole fourth grade."

"*I'm* one of the funniest kids in my grade," Annabelle boasted.

"Well, you girls can try to make them laugh," Vicki told them. "But I don't think you can do it. No one has before."

A little while later, the tour bus arrived near Buckingham Palace. Katie stared at the large white building in amazement. It was huge—nearly a whole block long. There were giant statues of people on horseback in front of the palace. And of course, the building was surrounded by a big black and gold gate, to protect the Queen and her family.

"Wow!" Katie exclaimed. "Is the Queen there now?"

"She is, indeed," Vicki assured her.

"How can you tell?" Mrs. Carew asked.

"Look up on the roof," Vicki said. "You see the royal banner? They only put that up when the Queen is staying there."

"So do you think she'll come outside?" Katie was still hoping to see the Queen in person.

"I wouldn't count on it," Annabelle said.

The bus stopped. One by one the people on the tour got off. They followed Vicki around the corner to the front gates of the palace. Sure enough, there were the guards, in their red tunics, big furry black hats, and black pants.

Almost immediately, the Garcias and the McIntyres began snapping pictures of one another. Mrs. Penderbottom ran off to buy some souvenir postcards. Miss Cornblau and Miss Framingham took notes, so they could tell their classes all about the changing of the guard. The Fishmans probably weren't going to see a thing. They weren't even looking at the palace. They were too busy staring at each other.

There were tons of other tourists standing in front of the Palace. They were snapping pictures and speaking in different languages.

Katie and Annabelle were in the middle of the crowd, near their parents. But Annabelle wanted a closer look.

"Katie, let's have a contest to see which of us can make that guard laugh first," she suggested. Annabelle pointed to a tall man standing in a guard box.

"Didn't you hear Vicki?" Katie reminded her. "The guards aren't *allowed* to laugh.

They have to stand still."

"But Vicki also said we could try and make them laugh if we wanted to," Annabelle noted. "So let's do it. We can make funny faces or tell jokes."

"I don't know," Katie interrupted. "It's kind of mean to try and make the guard laugh when he's not supposed to."

"Well," Annabelle said, "if you're *afraid* to try . . ."

Katie scowled. Annabelle was daring her to have this contest. If Katie said no, Annabelle would think she was a chicken. And Katie was *no* chicken.

"Okay, let's go," Katie said finally, pushing her way through the crowd and walking toward the guard. Annabelle followed close behind.

"Katie, don't go too far," her father called out.

"I'm just getting a better look," Katie assured him.

"Me too," Annabelle told her parents.

Finally, Katie and Annabelle reached the front of the crowd. Katie watched Annabelle stick her fingers just under her nose, and push her nostrils straight up. Then she stuck her tongue way out.

Katie had to admit it was a pretty funny face. But the guard didn't even seem to notice Annabelle.

Now it was Katie's turn. She thought for a minute. What was the funniest thing she could do? Hmmm . . . Once George had taught Katie how to imitate a monkey. Now *that* was really funny!

Katie shoved her tongue just under her top lip so it stuck out. Then she bent her arms and began scratching her armpit. "Ook ook," she said as she jumped around like a monkey.

The guard didn't crack a smile.

"That wasn't funny enough," Annabelle said.

"*You* didn't make him laugh, either," Katie reminded Annabelle.

"Maybe a joke will work," Annabelle suggested. She turned to the guard. "Do you know what kind of umbrella the Queen of England carries on a rainy day?"

The guard didn't answer, so Annabelle just finished the joke. "A wet one!" she announced.

Katie looked up at the guard's face. He was staring straight ahead. "He's not going to laugh," she told Annabelle.

"I guess not," Annabelle agreed. She reached down and pulled a yellow cardboard camera from her pocketbook. "I'll just take a few pictures."

"Where'd you get that?" Katie asked her.

"At the newsstand when we stopped to see Big Ben," Annabelle answered.

Katie would have loved to take photos to

show her grandma and her friends back home. But she hadn't thought to buy a camera when they were at Big Ben.

"Oh well. I guess I won't be able to take any pictures today," Katie sighed.

"Why not?" Annabelle asked her. "There's another newsstand right over there. A lot of the newsstands in London sell disposable cameras."

Katie ran to her parents. "Daddy," she asked, "could I buy a camera over at that newsstand?"

"I don't see why not," Mr. Carew said as he opened his wallet and pulled out a few of the multi-colored bills. "You have a few pounds here," he said, handing her the British money. "Be sure to get the change."

"I will," Katie assured him.

"And hurry," Vicki added. "They're going to have the changing of the guard ceremony shortly."

Katie raced as quickly as she could to the newsstand on the corner. Unfortunately, when she got there, the stand was closed.

Katie walked around the back of the stand. She was hoping to find the owner. Maybe he would open up his stand and sell her a camera. But there was no one around the back, either.

She stood there, all alone behind the newsstand, and sighed. She wasn't going to get a camera right now. Annabelle would probably never let her forget that.

Just then, Katie felt a slight breeze on the back of her neck. She pulled her jacket a little tighter around her. But that didn't help much. A little jean jacket was no match for the magic wind!

Before Katie knew what was happening, the wind began blowing full force. It spun around Katie like a wild tornado. Katie bit her lip and tried not to cry. Her mind was racing. What if the magic wind blew her to another country or something? How would she ever find her way back to her parents?

The wind swirled faster and harder. It seemed as though it would never stop.

And then, suddenly, it did. Just like that.

Switcheroo! Katie wasn't Katie anymore.

Chapter 3

Katie squeezed her eyes shut. She was afraid to open them. All around her she could hear people laughing and talking. A few babies were crying and some little kids were whining.

Where was she?

There was only one way to find out. She slowly opened her eyes. Lots of eyes stared back at her. She recognized two sets of eyes— the ones belonging to her parents. They were staring at her from a crowd. But they had no idea who she was.

Then again, neither did Katie.

Slowly, she looked down. Instead of her red

sneakers, Katie was wearing a pair of shiny black men's shoes. As her eyes traveled up, she saw a pair of pants, and a red jacket.

A bead of sweat formed on Katie's head. The jacket was too heavy for this weather. The hat on her head wasn't helping, either. She reached up and wiped the sweat from her forehead.

"Hey! I think I saw that guard move!"

Katie heard a familiar voice from the crowd. It was Annabelle's. And she was pointing right at Katie.

Oh, no! Now Katie knew why she was wearing such a heavy jacket and a hat. She'd turned into one of the Queen's guards!

Annabelle leaped out in front of the guard box. "I'll bet I can make him laugh now," she told her mother. She scrunched her lips and crossed her eyes.

It was a pretty funny face. But Katie didn't laugh. She didn't want to get the real guard in trouble. She didn't want to lose her bet with Annabelle, either.

"Annabelle, that's enough," Mrs. Bridgeman said. "He's not going to laugh. Let's just watch."

Annabelle didn't listen to her mother. Instead, she bent over and placed her hands on the ground. She rested her knees on her elbows, and then very, very slowly straightened her legs in the air.

"Everyone smiles when someone stands on her head," Annabelle said.

"Stop that!" her mother scolded her.

Boom! Annabelle wasn't very good at handstands. She flipped right over . . . and landed on her bottom!

Now *that* was funny! Katie couldn't hold back her laughter.

"Hey! That guard laughed!" Katie heard a man say.

"I saw him, too," a woman agreed. "They're not supposed to do that!"

"Lil! Get the camera!" Mr. McIntyre

shouted. "We've got to get a shot of this!"

Katie gulped. She had to stop laughing. Right *away*.

But that wasn't so easy. Once Katie got a case of the giggles, it was hard for her to hold them back.

Just then a marching band entered the yard. Immediately, the other guards switched positions. They turned, and began marching toward the palace.

A second group of guards lined up and began to march as well. The changing of the guard had begun.

Cameras began clicking wildly. All of the tourists who had gathered at the gates of the palace were taking pictures of the ceremony.

Katie gulped. She had no idea what to do. Where should she turn? Where could she go? She couldn't just run away. Not with all these people staring at her.

There was only one thing to do. She was going to have to try to follow what the other guards were doing.

One group of guards was marching toward the palace. The other was marching toward the gate. Katie wasn't sure which group she was supposed to march with. Finally, she clicked her heels together and joined the guards who were heading toward the front gate.

"What are you doing?" one of the guards whispered to Katie.

"I'm marching," she whispered back.

"You're supposed to be over there," the guard told her. "Your troop is leaving. We're the new ones coming in."

Oops. Katie had made a big mistake. Quickly, she turned and marched over toward the other end of the yard.

But she wasn't fast enough. Before Katie could reach the other line, the guards disappeared through a small door in the building.

Katie was left all alone in the middle of the yard. Everyone was staring at her. A few people started to point and chuckle.

Katie hated it when people stared at her. She hated it even more when people laughed at her. She was so upset, she forgot she was supposed to be a dignified guard at Buckingham Palace. Instead, she did what any fourth-grader would do.

She ran off and hid behind one of the large stone walls of the palace.

Phew. Katie breathed a sigh of relief. It felt good to be away from all those people staring at her. She adjusted the big, black furry hat and wiped the sweat from her face. Boy, those guards sure had a tough job. It wasn't easy standing there, perfectly still. Especially not when you were sweating under a jacket and a hat.

Just then, a gentle breeze began to blow. Katie was glad to feel a little wind blowing. The magic wind had returned.

And that meant Katie was in for another change.

The wind grew stronger and stronger,

circling around Katie wildly.

And then it stopped. Just like that. The magic wind was gone.

Slowly, Katie opened her eyes. She looked around. She wasn't inside the palace gates anymore. She was on the other side of the gate, looking in.

Katie glanced down at her feet. There were her red sneakers. She reached up to the top of her head. Her hands touched strands of her own red hair. The hat was gone.

"Katie, there you are!" Mrs. Carew shouted, rushing over to her daughter. "Did you get to see the changing of the guard?"

"I had a *really* close-up view," Katie assured her mom.

"Did you see me make that guard laugh?" Annabelle asked.

Katie nodded. "I'll bet he was really embarrassed about it."

Annabelle shrugged. "Whatever. I still won our bet."

Katie sighed. She couldn't believe Annabelle wasn't the least bit sorry for making the guard laugh in front of everyone. She had no idea what it felt like.

Then again, why would she? It was Katie who had turned into the guard.

And it was Katie who felt just awful about it.

Chapter 4

LAUGHING GUARD OUT OF STEP AT BUCKINGHAM PALACE

Katie stood in the lobby of her hotel and stared at the newspaper headline. Beneath the headline was a picture of the guard at Buckingham Palace. Even under his big hat you could see that he had a giant smile on his face.

Next to the picture was an article about how the guard had laughed at a little girl doing a handstand, and then had embarrassed the entire squad during the changing of the guard ceremony.

Except it wasn't really the guard who had

done that. It was Katie. And there was nothing she could do to make things better for him.

"So, are we ready for a morning of shopping?" Mrs. Carew asked Katie.

Katie sighed. A morning of shopping with her parents didn't seem like a whole lot of fun.

"Hi there!" Vicki greeted the Carew family as she came bounding into the lobby. She glanced at Katie. "Why the long face, mate?"

"Katie doesn't feel like shopping," Mr. Carew explained.

Vicki nodded. "Well, how about Katie and I go to Hyde Park today, while you go to Harrods Department Store?"

Katie brightened. Maybe being in the park would make her feel better about everything.

"I'm taking Annabelle, too," Vicki continued.

Or maybe it wouldn't.

"That's not a bad idea," Katie's mother agreed.

"Super," Vicki said. "It's settled. Annabelle

should be down any minute. And then we're off to the park."

"We have a park like this in Boston," Annabelle boasted as she, Vicki, and Katie walked through the beautiful grassy gardens in Hyde Park.

"Really," Vicki replied. She stopped for a minute so the girls could look out over a big lake.

"It's called the Boston Common and . . ." Annabelle began.

"What's this lake called?" Katie interrupted as they stopped to watch people row boats across the water.

"Serpentine Lake," Vicki told her. "People come from all over London to go boating. In the summer, people swim here."

"I'm kind of tired," Annabelle moaned. "Do you think we could rest?"

Katie frowned. Annabelle wasn't happy unless she was talking about Boston.

"Of course," Vicki said. "You two go over to those benches. I'll get us some ice cream."

"I like chocolate best," Annabelle told her.

"How about you, Katie?" Vicki asked.

"I like strawberry," Katie told her. "Thanks, Vicki."

"Two ice-cream cones," Vicki repeated. "Coming right up."

As Vicki walked off, Katie and Annabelle wandered over toward the benches.

"So, do you like living in Cherrydale?" Annabelle asked Katie.

"Oh yeah," Katie replied. "I have a lot of friends there."

"Have you lived there your whole life?"

Katie nodded.

"That must be nice," Annabelle said. "I haven't lived in any place for very long. My dad's job is always changing. So far I've lived in Chicago, Orlando, New York, and now Boston. I really like Boston. I have a lot of friends there."

"That's good," Katie replied.

"Not really," Annabelle replied. "We're moving again. To Houston, Texas. I'm going to have to make all new friends."

Suddenly Katie understood why Annabelle had been talking about Boston so much. She loved it there. And she didn't want to leave.

"Houston will be great," Katie assured her, kindly. "You'll learn to talk with a southern accent."

"It *is* a cool accent," Annabelle agreed. She smiled at Katie. Then she turned her eyes toward a man on a bench a few feet away from them. He was wearing a black baseball cap and a red shirt. He was eating a sandwich from a brown paper bag. "I think I've seen that guy before," she told Katie.

Katie looked over at the man. "Maybe he's staying at the same hotel."

Annabelle shook her head. "No. That's not it." She hopped off the bench.

"Where are you going?" Katie asked her.

"To find out who he is."

Katie knew better than to talk to strangers. "That's a bad idea," she said.

Annabelle didn't care. She got up and

walked straight toward the mystery man.

Katie couldn't let her do that alone. It was too dangerous. "Annabelle, wait!" she cried out as she ran after her.

Chapter 5

Annabelle was quick. By the time Katie caught up to her, she was already seated next to the man on the bench.

"Do I know you?" Annabelle asked.

The man pulled his baseball hat farther down his face. "I doubt it," he said in a thick English accent.

Annabelle stared even harder. "You're that guard from Buckingham Palace!" she exclaimed. "The one *I* made laugh."

The man sat up suddenly. He glared at Annabelle. "That was *you*?"

Annabelle nodded proudly. "Don't you remember me?"

The man frowned. "I guess so. It's all kind of foggy."

"What was it about me that made you laugh when no one else could?" Annabelle asked him.

"I don't know. I didn't . . ." he began.

"Yes, you did," Annabelle told him. "Everyone saw you."

"Don't remind me," the man answered her.

"Did you get in trouble?" Katie asked nervously.

"You can't make mistakes when you're guarding the Queen," he answered with a sigh. "I'm on desk duty from now on. No more fancy uniforms. No more marching. It's not the way I wanted to go out."

"Go out?" Katie asked.

"I'm almost finished with my time in the guard," he explained.

"Oh," Katie said. "So what are you going to do next?"

"I don't know," the guard told her. "I don't think anyone would hire me. I'm a real laughingstock."

At that moment, Vicki came over. "Girls, you shouldn't just disappear like that," she scolded them. "I think you know better than to talk to strangers. Come on, girls. Let's go." She handed the girls their ice-cream cones.

"He's not a stranger," Annabelle told her. "This is the guard from the palace. The one *I* made laugh."

"Oh. I see." The tour guide held out her hand. "I'm Vicki."

"Tim Becker," the guard replied.

"He's going to leave the guard soon," Katie told Vicki. "We're talking about the jobs he could have."

"Girls," Vicki said. "I don't think . . ."

But Katie really wanted to help Tim. She *had* to. "Wasn't there something you wanted to do before this all happened?"

Tim thought for a moment. "Well, there was one thing. But . . . oh, never mind. You'll think I've gone bonkers."

"No, we won't," Katie insisted.

"Well," Tim said slowly, "I've always wanted to be a stand-up comic. All my mates say I'm the funniest bloke they know."

"Have you ever tried doing stand-up comedy?" Vicki asked him.

"Not really," Tim answered. "Although everyone's laughing at me now, anyway."

Katie frowned. She felt just awful about that.

Then, suddenly she got one of her great ideas. "If everyone's laughing anyway, why don't you do an act in a club?"

"It's not that easy," Tim told her. "You can't just walk into a club and say you want to go onstage."

"Actually you can," Vicki told him. "There's a place right near Piccadilly Circus that has amateur night. Anyone can try to be a comic there."

"But I don't have an act," Tim said.

"Sure you do," Katie told him. She was getting excited now. "You could talk about all the funny things people do to make the guards laugh at Buckingham Palace."

Tim thought for a moment. "You tourists do look pretty funny from our point of view," he said with a chuckle.

"You can use my joke about the umbrella if you want," Annabelle suggested.

Katie sighed. Annabelle would never change. But maybe Tim's life would.

Two nights later, Katie sat in the small, dark comedy club. Her parents were there. So was the Bridgeman family. Vicki had brought a few other members of the tour group, too, just to be sure that Tim had an audience.

But they didn't really need to do that. One of the local radio stations had found out that the "Laughing Guard" was going to try to make other people laugh for a change. They had announced the time and place for the show. The club was mobbed. And not just with customers. There were a few news crews there, too.

Katie was scared. What if Tim wasn't funny? He'd be all over the news making a fool out of himself. And it would all be Katie's fault . . . *again*!

Suddenly, a loud booming voice announced, "Ladies and Gentlemen . . . here he is . . . Tim Becker!"

Tim walked onto the stage. But he didn't say anything. Instead, he started making really weird faces. He stuck his tongue out, crossed his eyes, and did a goofy dance.

The audience laughed really hard.

Tim grinned. "That's what the world looks like to me," he told them. "Just a bunch of people making faces. *You* try not laughing at that."

He made a few more faces. The audience laughed even harder. It was impossible not to. Tim was really funny. Even the reporters were laughing!

Katie smiled proudly. Tim was a hit! His dream was coming true. And he had Katie to thank for it. Well, actually, Katie *and* the magic wind. But there was no way Katie was giving any credit to that wind!

Dear Suzanne,

Bonjour! (That means hello in French.) You would love Paris. The women all dress really fancy, with pearls and scarves. We got to visit a nearby factory where they made perfume. It smelled so good!

Au revoir (that means good-bye)!
Wish you were here,
Katie

Suzanne Locke
Cherrydale
USA

Chapter 6

"Oh my goodness!" Katie gasped. She was looking down from the observation deck high up in the Eiffel Tower. Her tour group had had to wait in line a long time until they got into the elevator at the bottom of the tower. Now they were squished together with lots and lots of other tourists on the deck. But it was all worth it. "I can see all of Paris from here. We're up so high!" she exclaimed.

Vicki nodded. "It's 1,652 stairs to the top!"

"I'm sure glad we didn't have to *walk* up all those stairs!" Annabelle said.

"Me too," Katie said. "I just can't believe how beautiful Paris looks from up here!"

"It really is an amazing view," Mrs. Penderbottom agreed. "But not as incredible as the Louvre art museum. I just loved seeing the *Mona Lisa*."

"I thought the *Mona Lisa* was really small," Annabelle said. "We have paintings in the art museum in Boston that are much larger."

Katie rolled her eyes.

"There are paintings in the Louvre that are larger, too," Vicki reminded her. "But none more famous."

"It's not about the size of the painting," Mr. Penderbottom explained. "It's about the talent and skill in the work."

"I loved Mona Lisa's smile," Mr. Fishman said. "It reminded me of my wife's." He gave his bride a peck on the cheek.

Ew! Katie and Annabelle both looked away.

"I'm hungry," Annabelle said suddenly. She turned to Vicki. "Didn't you say there was a restaurant in the Eiffel Tower?"

Vicki nodded. "There is. But I think you'd have more fun eating the way real Parisians do. They can spend a whole afternoon sitting at a café watching people go by."

"That sounds like fun," Katie said.

"It *is* fun," Annabelle agreed. "We have a really cool outdoor café near my house in Boston. I go there all the time for lunch."

Katie rolled her eyes again.

"You know, I could go for one of those ham and cheese sandwiches I saw people eating yesterday," Mr. Carew suggested.

Annabelle's father nodded. "Me too." He turned to Vicki. "Can you recommend a good café?"

"There's one right near the Cathedral of Notre Dame," Vicki said. "That's the next stop on our tour of Paris."

"Notre Dame," Katie squealed excitedly. "Do you think we'll see the Hunchback?"

"That's only in the movies," Annabelle told her.

Katie frowned. Annabelle was such a know-it-all.

"That's true," Vicki agreed. She smiled at Katie. "But I think you'll like Notre Dame anyway. There's no other place like it."

Annabelle opened her mouth to speak, but Katie beat her to it.

"Not even in Boston?" Katie asked Vicki.

Annabelle blushed.

Vicki laughed. "Not in the whole world," she assured Katie.

Chapter 7

Vicki wasn't kidding. The Cathedral of Notre Dame was amazing! It was also kind of scary. The old church was decorated with huge, creepy stone monsters called gargoyles. They stuck out from the outer walls of the building, glaring angrily at the people on the street below.

The grown-up tourists seemed really interested in the gargoyles. The Garcias and the McIntyres were even taking pictures of one another making creepy faces. But Katie thought the stone creatures were really scary.

"I don't like those things," Katie said with a shiver. She turned away from the monsters' rock-hard stares.

"They're really just water spouts," Vicki assured her.

"*Creepy* water spouts," Katie corrected the tour guide.

Suddenly Katie heard a loud rumbling. *"AAAAHHH!"* she screamed out. She grabbed her mother by the arm. "What was that?"

"It was just my stomach growling," Annabelle said with a giggle.

"I think she's hungry," Mrs. Bridgeman told Vicki. "Didn't you say there was a café nearby?"

Vicki pointed toward the street. "There's one right on the corner there. The girls will love it."

Katie was happy when she and her parents began to follow the Bridgemans away from the cathedral. She couldn't wait to leave those gargoyles!

✕　✕　✕

"I would like a *fromage* sandwich," Katie

told the waiter at the café. She smiled proudly as she used the French word for cheese. The waiter smiled back and wrote down her order.

Then the waiter walked over to the next small table where Annabelle and her parents were sitting. The tables at the café were so small that they couldn't all sit together. But they were close enough.

"Ruff! Ruff!"

Katie turned around. The woman at the next table was sitting with a small black poodle on her lap. In Paris, lots of restaurants allowed dogs to sit at the table.

Pepper would love that, Katie thought to herself. She missed her cocker spaniel. He was back home in Cherrydale. Katie's next-door neighbors, Mr. and Mrs. Derkman, were taking care of him while the Carews were away. Katie hoped Mrs. Derkman was being nicer to Pepper than she had been to her third-grade class. When Mrs. Derkman had been Katie's teacher, she'd been really strict.

"Do you think Pepper's okay?" Katie asked her mother.

"I'm sure he's fine, Katie," Mrs. Carew answered. "He's probably busy playing with Snowball in the yard right now."

Snowball was Mrs. Derkman's dog. She was Pepper's best friend . . . other than Katie, of course.

"I think I'll send Pepper a postcard," Katie told her mother. "I saw one with a picture of a French poodle on it back at the hotel."

Mrs. Carew smiled. "I think Pepper would like that."

Just then the waiter arrived with coffee for the adults and sodas for Annabelle and Katie.

"*Merci,*" Katie said, proudly using the French word for thank you.

As she sipped her soda, Katie looked out at the street. People were walking by. Mothers with strollers. Businesspeople with leather briefcases. A dog walker with six large dogs pulling her down the street.

Vicki was right. It was fun to people-watch in Paris.

Katie could see Notre Dame from her seat at the café. It didn't look nearly as scary from here. In fact, it looked kind of pretty.

A group of artists were seated across the street on small wooden folding chairs. Each artist had set up a small easel. Katie watched as their hands glided across their canvases. Some seemed to be using paint, while others were drawing with pencils. They were all looking up at Notre Dame as they worked.

"They're painting the cathedral," Katie said. "It looks like fun. Daddy, do you have a pen?"

Mr. Carew pulled a pen from his shirt pocket. "Here you go," he told her.

Katie took the pen and began to draw on her napkin. She looked up at the cathedral and tried to get the points in the tower just right. It was really hard to do.

Annabelle looked over to see what Katie was doing. "Oh, I want to try that, too," Annabelle said.

Mrs. Bridgeman pulled a pen from her purse and handed it to her daughter. Before long, both girls were busy drawing.

Katie loved everything about Paris. It was such fun sitting at an outdoor café, drawing one of the most famous buildings in the whole world. She was speaking French (okay, so maybe she only knew a couple of words, but *still* . . .), and she was about to eat a *fromage* sandwich on real French bread.

Katie grinned broadly. It didn't get better than this!

Chapter 8

"Mmm. That was good," Mr. Bridgeman said as he finished the last of his french fries. "Anyone for another cup of coffee?"

"That sounds great," Mrs. Carew agreed.

Annabelle and Katie looked at each other and frowned. The girls were getting tired of sitting. Luckily, Annabelle had a better idea.

"Can Katie and I go see what those artists are drawing?" Annabelle asked.

"Well . . ." Mrs. Bridgeman began slowly.

"Come on, Mom. It's just across the street," Annabelle pleaded.

"I guess it's okay," she said. Then she looked at Katie's mother. "If it's fine with you."

Mrs. Carew nodded. "Just be careful crossing the street. The people in Paris drive a lot faster than people in Cherrydale."

"Oh, I can help her," Annabelle boasted. "These drivers are nothing compared to the cab drivers in Boston."

Katie scowled. She did *not* need any help crossing the street.

"And stay where we can see you," Mr. Carew said.

"I promise," Katie agreed.

"Come on," Annabelle urged as she leaped up from the table and headed toward the crosswalk. "I want to see how good their paintings are."

Apparently, Annabelle did not think the paintings were very good at all. As she and Katie stood behind the artists, watching them work, Annabelle began to laugh.

"*My* drawing was better than these," she said. "These don't even *look* like Notre Dame."

"Annabelle!" Katie exclaimed. "That's not very nice."

"Oh, don't worry about it. They don't even know what we're saying," Annabelle assured Katie. "They speak French, not English, remember?"

Katie sighed. That didn't make a difference. "Well, anyway, I don't think these are supposed to look exactly like the cathedral."

"They don't look *anything* like it,"

Annabelle insisted. "I did better art than this in kindergarten."

Katie was really glad the artists didn't speak English. Their feelings would be hurt if they knew what Annabelle was actually saying.

The girls moved behind the last artist in the row. He was covered in paint. There were colorful stains on his slacks, shirt, and even his shoes. At the moment he was busy drawing squares and triangles with a charcoal pencil. His hands moved quickly as he sketched.

"See what I mean?" Annabelle asked her.

Katie shrugged. "Well, I did draw a lot of shapes in kindergarten," she agreed. "And some of my pictures looked a *little* like that."

Suddenly, the artist whipped around in his chair. "Do you think I cannot understand you?" he shouted in a thick French accent. "I speak English very well!"

Katie gasped. Her cheeks turned as red as her hair. "I . . . I'm sorry," she murmured. "I didn't . . ."

"You don't know anything about art. You are just foolish children. Now go away! Scat, like little cats!" the artist shouted at them.

Katie did as she was told. Without even waiting for Annabelle, she ran off into a nearby alleyway.

The alley was filled with wooden vegetable crates. A few rotting cabbages littered the ground. They stunk really badly. They smelled as badly as Pepper did that time a skunk had sprayed him.

Katie guessed she deserved to be in a stinky alleyway. After all, she and Annabelle had said some pretty mean things about the artist who had been drawing shapes on his canvas. This was sort of like her punishment.

She sat down on a hard wooden crate. Maybe if she waited here long enough, the artist would leave. Then she could walk back out onto the sidewalk and go across the street to the café where her parents were sitting.

But deep down Katie knew she was going

to have to walk out there and see him again. If the artist yelled at her, she would just have to listen. And say she was sorry—*again*.

Katie stood up and got ready to walk out of the alley. But before she could take even one step, a cool breeze began to blow.

Within seconds the breeze grew stronger. Soon it felt more like a wind than a breeze. And not just any wind. *This was the magic wind!*

Before Katie knew what was happening, the magic wind was circling wildly around her. Katie grabbed onto one of the crates and held on tight. The tornado was really wild this time. She shut her eyes tight, and tried not to cry.

And then it stopped. Just like that.

The magic wind was gone. And so was Katie Carew.

Chapter 9

Katie sniffed the air. She didn't smell any rotten cabbages. Obviously, she wasn't in the alley anymore.

So where was she?

Slowly, Katie opened her eyes and looked around. She could see her parents sitting at the café across the street, happily enjoying their coffee. She breathed a sigh of relief. At least she hadn't gone far. Katie didn't know her way around Paris. It was good to know that her parents were nearby.

Now Katie knew *where* she was. But she still didn't know *who* she was. Slowly she looked down at her hands. They were large and kind of hairy. *They were a man's hands!*

Okay, she was a man. But *what* man?

Maybe her clothes could give her a clue. She was wearing loose-fitting, blue cotton pants. They were stained with different colored paints. So was her white T-shirt. There were little spots of colored paints on her black leather shoes.

Uh-oh. Katie had turned into a street artist. And not just any artist. Katie had become the artist she and Annabelle had been making fun of!

She sat there for a minute, staring at the painting and wishing that the magic wind would return and change her back. But deep down she knew that was impossible. The magic wind only came when Katie was alone. Right now she was on a busy street.

The other artists certainly were painting very quickly. Once in a while they would glance up at the sky and frown.

Katie followed their glances. The sky was

getting pretty dark, and it looked like it was about to rain.

Uh-oh, Katie thought again.

The artist sitting beside Katie reached over and took a tube of paint from the box of art supplies beside her easel.

"Okay, Pierre?" the artist asked Katie in a heavy French accent.

Well, at least she knew his name. Katie Carew was now Pierre. Unfortunately that was *all* she knew. She had absolutely no idea how to finish the painting in front of her.

But if she didn't finish it, Pierre wouldn't be able to sell his painting. That was how he made a living. Katie had to try. She owed him at least that much.

Katie figured Pierre probably had been trying to paint Notre Dame. After all, he'd been staring at the cathedral as he worked. But to Katie, his canvas just looked like a mess of charcoal-pencil triangles, rectangles, and squares.

Katie decided to begin painting in the shapes. She was pretty sure she could do that. Katie was very good at staying in the lines when she painted. She'd been doing that since first grade.

She picked up a paintbrush, and looked down at the tubes of paint Pierre had arranged so neatly beside his drawing. *Hmmm.* Which one should she start with? Finally, she picked up a tube of red paint and squirted a little bit into the center of one of the squares.

Wow! That was a really bright red. Katie liked it a lot. She began to move the paint around with the brush, filling in the square perfectly.

Then she picked up another paintbrush and squirted a blob of yellow paint onto the big triangle at the top of the canvas.

Katie began to relax. Painting was a lot of fun. And as long as her parents and the Bridgemans stayed across the street drinking coffee, Katie didn't have to worry about being lost or alone in Paris.

As she colored in a blue square, Katie noticed Annabelle peering out from behind a nearby pole. She obviously didn't want the artists to see her. She must have felt badly about making fun of Pierre's painting, just like Katie had.

The artist sitting next to Katie turned to take a peek at what she was doing on her canvas. Katie leaned back to give him a good look.

Katie thought her painting was nice. Maybe even better than the ones the real artists had done. Their canvases all were covered with gloomy gray, brown, and black paint. They all looked pretty much the same.

But Katie's painting was bright and cheerful—all reds, yellows, greens, and blues. She thought it would make people smile.

And she was right. The other artists did all smile . . . and *then they started to laugh*. They were making fun of her!

Katie was really angry. She threw down her paintbrush and jumped up from her chair.

"You guys are so mean!" she exclaimed.

The artists all looked at her strangely.

They didn't understand what she was saying. But Annabelle did.

"You don't have to get so mad," she said as she peeked her head out from behind the pole.

Katie scowled. Annabelle was wrong. She *did* have a right to be mad. Nobody liked being made fun of.

But Katie didn't feel like explaining that to Annabelle right then. All she wanted to do was get out of there. She really needed to be alone.

Katie stormed off toward the alleyway where she'd hidden before. It smelled just awful. But as far as Katie was concerned, being around stinky cabbages was better than being with Annabelle and the artists!

Chapter 10

Katie plopped down on a wooden crate and wiped a tear from her cheek. She had a lot to feel awful about. She'd hurt Pierre's feelings. And the other artists had laughed at her painting. But worst of all, her parents would soon be finished with lunch. They were going to come looking for her any minute.

Katie was going to be in big trouble. Her parents had told her to stay where they could see her. But now, when they looked for Katie, all they'd see was an artist with paint-stained shoes.

And Annabelle was probably wondering where she was, too. After all, Katie had just run off without her.

Katie really wanted to be herself again.
Where was the magic wind when she needed it?

Just then, Katie felt a familiar breeze blowing on the back of her neck. It grew stronger
and stronger, blowing all around Katie like a
tornado.

And then it stopped.

Katie looked down at her feet. The paint-
stained shoes had been replaced by Katie's red
high-top sneakers. And she was back in her
own purple cargo pants and pink T-shirt.

Woohoo! She was Katie Carew!

Now her parents wouldn't be angry with
her for disappearing. Her big problem was
solved!

That was more than Pierre could say. As
Katie peered out from the alleyway, she could
see him sitting in his chair. He was staring at
the red, green, blue, and yellow canvas. He
looked kind of confused . . . and very upset.

Katie felt really bad for him. She really

wanted to cheer him up.

"Oh, I like that," Katie said, walking over toward Pierre.

"You, again!" he shouted. "Didn't I tell you to go away?"

"But I like your painting," Katie assured him.

"It's not *my* painting," he told her.

"Yes, it is. I saw you working on it," Annabelle called out from her hiding place behind the pole.

"I didn't paint . . ." Pierre sighed and shook his head. "Or maybe I did. I don't know. I can't really remember."

"It's really different from everyone else's paintings," Katie told him.

"It's a mess," Pierre replied. "I don't know what made me use these colors."

"If you don't like it, why don't you just get a new canvas and start over?" Annabelle asked him.

"Canvases are expensive," Pierre told her.

"I have to sell this painting before I can buy the paints and canvas. I will need to do another one." He sighed. "But I don't see how I'm going to sell this."

His friends obviously didn't think he would sell it either. They were all pointing at his artwork and laughing.

Katie really wished she could help him. But how?

Then, suddenly, she remembered something Ms. Barnes, her art teacher at school, had taught her.

"Maybe you could add some white or black to a few of the shapes," she suggested. "Then you'll have different shades of the colors."

"You think I don't know that?" Pierre asked her. "I'm an artist. I know how to change colors. But these are not colors I would want at all. I'm painting Notre Dame. It should be gray and black."

"It doesn't look like Notre Dame," Annabelle said. "It looks like squares and triangles."

Pierre rolled his eyes. "Foolish child. This is abstract art. It's not supposed to look like Notre Dame. But it *is* supposed to be dark and gloomy."

"Why?" Katie asked him. "Everyone does it that way. I think it's great that you did something different. Sometimes change can be good."

Pierre shrugged. "I suppose," he said slowly. "It's worth a try. Maybe I can save this after all." He put a dab of white paint in the middle of a blue square and began to swirl it around with his paintbrush.

"Oh, that's pretty," Katie said as she watched the bright blue become lighter. It looked just like the color of the sky.

"It's not bad," Pierre agreed. He added a touch of gray paint to Katie's red triangle. "Not bad at all."

Chapter 11

Katie and Annabelle watched as Pierre finished the painting. He worked quickly, changing the shades of several of the colors. He sketched in a few more shapes and painted them in.

As Pierre put the finishing strokes on his canvas, the girls' parents walked across the street.

"Did you have a good time?" Mr. Carew asked as he came up beside Katie.

She nodded. "We're watching Pierre finish his painting of Notre Dame."

Pierre looked at her strangely. "How do you know my name?"

Katie gulped. *How was she going to explain this one?*

"It says Pierre right there, on your paint box," Annabelle pointed out.

Katie breathed a sigh of relief. *Phew.* That had been close.

Mr. Bridgeman looked at the artists' easels. Most of the men leaned back to give him a better view of their work. Pierre leaned forward. He didn't want anyone seeing this painting.

But it was Pierre's artwork that Mr. Bridgeman focused on the longest. "This is very interesting," he said. "I haven't seen any-thing like it."

"Well, it's not my best work . . ." Pierre began.

"I think it's fantastic," Mrs. Bridgeman interrupted him. "It's just what I was looking for. I need a cheerful painting like this for my new house in Houston."

"You use wonderful colors," Mr.

Bridgeman told Pierre. "They're so bright."

"It's a change for me," Pierre told the Bridgemans. "And change can be good." He winked at Katie. Katie winked back.

The other artists watched as Mr. and Mrs. Bridgeman talked about how much the painting would cost. The Bridgemans were paying for it in Euros, the kind of money a lot of countries in Europe use.

Katie had no idea how much the painting cost in American dollars. But it must have been expensive, because the other artists seemed really impressed. They weren't laughing at Pierre anymore. One of the men even splashed a big blob of yellow paint onto the center of his gray, black, and brown painting.

"You're so lucky," Katie told Annabelle. "You're going to have one of Pierre's paintings in your new house."

"I'd rather have it in my old house . . . and stay in Boston," Annabelle said with a heavy sigh.

"It will be okay," Katie assured her. "You heard what Pierre said. Change can be good."

"That's easy for you to say," Annabelle replied. "Nothing ever changes for you."

Katie thought about all the changes the magic wind had brought her on this vacation. "That's what you think," she murmured.

Dear Emma W.,
Hola! (That means hello in Spanish.) This is a picture of the public gardens in Madrid, Spain. I saw a puppet show there. I didn't understand a lot of it because it was in Spanish. But the show was still really funny. The puppets kept hitting each other on the head.
    Wish you were here!
    Katie

Emma Weber
Cherrydale
USA

Chapter 12

"Are there really four *thousand* animals here?" Katie asked Vicki as they entered the Faunia, a giant zoo in Madrid.

"It looks like there are at least four thousand people here," Mrs. Garcia noted. "This certainly is a popular tourist attraction."

Katie looked around. Mrs. Garcia was right. There were crowds of people everywhere. Many of them were studying giant maps of Faunia.

Vicki nodded. "Faunia is a super place," she said. "You can visit the whole world in one afternoon."

"I always wanted to take a trip around the world," Mr. McIntyre joked.

"And you will," Vicki assured him. "Today we will visit a tropical rain forest, walk around in the dark with bats flying around, and hang out with penguins in the South Pole."

"I love penguins," Annabelle squealed. "They walk so funny."

"I know," Katie agreed. She put her heels together and started to waddle around like a penguin. Annabelle did a penguin walk of her own.

"Quick, take out the camera," Mrs. Garcia shouted to her husband. "Get a good shot of the girls acting like penguins."

Mr. Garcia took photos of Katie and Annabelle as they waddled around.

"I can do that, too!" Mrs. McIntyre joked. "Look at me. I'm a penguin." She waddled over toward her husband.

"I guess we'll go to the South Pole part of the park first," Vicki told the group. "You folks should feel right at home there."

"I can't believe the Penderbottoms, Miss Cornblau, and Miss Framingham went to an art museum instead of coming here," Annabelle said. "This is so much fun!"

"The Prado is a pretty incredible art museum," Mrs. Carew told her. "It's got an amazing collection of paintings and sculptures by famous Spanish artists."

"I'd rather be around animals than just about anything," Annabelle told her.

Katie was happy to find that she and Annabelle had something in common. "I want to see all of the animals, even the bats!" she announced.

"Don't forget about the snakes in the rain forest," Annabelle added.

"I love snakes," Katie assured her. "We have one in our classroom. His name is Slinky."

"We have a turtle in our class," Annabelle said. "A snake would be so much cooler."

Katie was shocked. But not that Annabelle

had a turtle for a class pet. Katie was surprised that for once Annabelle wasn't bragging that what she had was the best.

This was going to be *una buena día*—a good day. Katie could just tell.

Chapter 13

Katie was right. Faunia was the greatest animal park she'd ever seen. The rain forest had been especially incredible—all warm and steamy. She'd seen birds whose bright colors were as beautiful as the rain-forest flowers. In fact, everything in the rain-forest exhibit was beautiful . . . even the lizards!

Annabelle, on the other hand, liked the penguins the best. "Those penguins were hysterical!" she giggled as they left the park. "I liked when they went sliding around on the ice."

"I really felt like I was in the South Pole," Katie agreed. "It was freezing in there!"

"I'm glad we got our picture taken with those parrots on our shoulders," Annabelle noted.

"Me too. I'm going to put mine on the bulletin board in my room," Katie assured her.

"I'll have to hang it in my *new* room," Annabelle told Katie. She sounded sad.

Katie knew just how to cheer her up. Nothing made Annabelle happier than eating!

"Vicki, can we stop for a snack?" Katie asked as the tour group left the park.

"Absolutely," Vicki replied. "And I know just the place!"

$\times$ $\times$ $\times$

Vicki had the bus driver bring the group to a café on Cava de San Miguel, a street that was built back in the Middle Ages! The adults all ordered fried pockets of dough filled with beef. Katie and Annabelle asked for fruit salad instead.

"I can't believe how old this street is,"

Katie said as she looked around. "A real knight could have been standing right here once upon a time."

"Maybe a princess rode by on her horse," Annabelle added. She waved her hand like a princess greeting her royal subjects.

"It would be so cool if we were wearing costumes like people wore back then," Katie remarked.

"You mean like those?" Mr. Garcia said as he took out his camera. Katie turned around in her chair. A group of street musicians were heading their way. They were dressed in long black capes and bright yellow sashes.

"Oh, here comes a tuna!" Vicki exclaimed as the waiter put a platter on the table.

Katie looked at her strangely. "I thought you said these fried sandwiches were filled with meat, not fish."

Vicki laughed. "No, not tuna *fish*, Katie. That group of street musicians is called a *tuna*. The musicians in a *tuna* are called *tunos. Tuna* groups have played music on the streets of Madrid for hundreds of years."

Katie giggled. "Oops."

The strolling musicians played their song as they traveled down Cava de San Miguel. They stopped as they reached the café where Katie and her tour group were sitting. One of the tambourine players walked over to Katie and reached for her hand.

Katie jumped back.

"It's okay," Vicki assured her. "He just wants you to dance."

Katie blushed. She didn't want to dance right in the middle of the street. Not in front of all these people!

But Annabelle did. She leaped up from her chair and began swaying back and forth to the music. "Come on, Katie," she urged. "It's fun."

Katie watched Annabelle. She did seem to be having a good time. Slowly she stood up to join her.

Annabelle grinned and curtsied low. Katie curtsied back. Then the girls began to dance wildly, right in the middle of the street.

Katie laughed.

"What's so funny?" Annabelle asked her.

"I'll never be able to look at a can of tuna fish again without thinking about dancing," Katie told her.

"Me either," Annabelle said with a laugh as she twirled around again.

When the *tuna* finished playing their song, the grown-ups all reached into their pockets and gave them some change.

"Well, that was fun," Mr. Bridgeman said as they got up to leave. "What a busy day. I sure am ready for my siesta now."

"Your *what*?" Annabelle asked him.

"My siesta. That's a mid-afternoon rest," Mr. Bridgeman told her. "And you girls should take one, too. That way you'll be fresh and ready for the bull fight this evening."

Katie gulped. "Bull fight?" she asked nervously.

"We're going to a bull fight?" Annabelle asked. She didn't sound any happier about it than Katie did.

"Yes," Vicki told her. "I got tickets for our whole group."

Katie frowned. She didn't want to go to a bull fight. She didn't want to see a man with a red cape and a sword hurt a poor bull.

Mrs. Carew studied her daughter's face. "I don't think Katie would like that very much," she said.

"Me either," Annabelle piped up.

"Well, there is something else you could do that would be a lot of fun," Vicki suggested. "You could go to a *tablao*."

"A *what*?" Katie asked.

"A *tablao*. That's a club where you can watch a flamenco dance show," Vicki explained. "I know of a place near the Plaza Mayor where you can have a delicious dinner and see a show."

"That sounds like fun," Mr. Carew said. "Annabelle, would you like to go to the *tablao* with us tonight instead?"

"Can I?" Annabelle asked her parents.

"It's fine with us," Mrs. Bridgeman agreed.

"Yeah!" the girls both cheered at once. Then they began dancing in the street again.

"Come on, you two," Mrs. Carew said as they headed toward the tour bus. "Even dancers need a siesta."

"A siesta resta!" Katie joked.

"Siesta resta. Siesta resta," Annabelle repeated. "It's like a song."

The girls sang and danced all the way down the street—just like a pair of *tunos*!

Chapter 14

After a nice long siesta, the Carew family
and Annabelle took a taxi to the *tablao*.

When Katie walked into the club, she had
a hard time seeing. It was so dark in there!
And crowded and noisy, too. Already, there
were lots of people seated at tables. Waiters
walked around with heavy trays filled with
big dishes of what looked like rice and soup.

A woman came up to them and led them to
a table.

"Mmm. The paella smells delicious," Mr.
Carew said.

"What's paella?" Katie asked.

"It's a Spanish dish made with rice,

vegetables, seafood, and meats," Mrs. Carew explained. She looked at her menu. "But they have vegetarian paella, too."

"I'll have that," Katie told her mother.

"Me too," Annabelle said.

"Do you girls want to start with gazpacho?" Mrs. Carew asked. "That's a delicious Spanish tomato vegetable soup."

"I'll try it," Annabelle said.

"Me too," Katie agreed. It was a little chilly in the club. A bowl of soup would be nice.

When the waiter came, Katie's mother ordered for the table. She was the only one of them who could speak any Spanish. She'd learned the language in college.

A few moments later, the waiter arrived with four big bowls of tomato soup on his tray.

"Boy, am I hungry," Mr. Carew said.

"Me too," Katie agreed. She took her spoon and scooped up a bit of soup. She bent down for a taste. "Hey, this soup is cold!" she said, surprised.

"Gazpacho is served cold," her mother said.

Annabelle stuck her spoon into the bowl. "I thought you said there were going to be vegetables in here."

"There will be," Mrs. Carew assured her.

Sure enough, the waiter placed four more bowls on the table. Each one was filled with pieces of fresh cucumbers, tomatoes, onions, and green peppers.

"You add your own vegetables," Mrs. Carew explained to the girls.

Katie put a big spoonful of tomatoes into her soup. "My friend Kevin would love this," she told Annabelle. "He's a tomato freak! He's trying to break the tomato-eating record."

"That's neat," Annabelle said. "We have a girl in my school who tried to break a record for hopping on one foot. She didn't break the record, but she almost broke her ankle."

Katie laughed. "She sounds like my friend

Suzanne. Once, she tried to break the record for walking backward—and she knocked over a clothing stand in the middle of the Cherrydale Mall."

"Even though you live in the suburbs and I live in the city, we have a lot of the same kinds of friends," Annabelle said.

"Kids are pretty much the same everywhere, I guess," Katie agreed. "That's why you shouldn't worry so much about moving to Houston. You'll make lots of new friends there."

Annabelle shrugged. "Maybe."

"Hey, you made a new friend in Europe, didn't you?" Katie continued.

"I did?" Annabelle asked. "Who?"

"Me, silly," Katie told her.

Annabelle smiled and picked up her water glass. "To friends," she said.

Katie clinked her glass against Annabelle's. "To friends," she echoed.

"That paella was yummy," Annabelle said a while later as the waiter picked up her empty plate. "I am *so* full."

"Me too," Katie agreed, patting her stomach and leaning back in her chair.

From her seat, Katie could see the dancers warming up backstage. The women were all wearing elegant costumes. Most of the dresses were brightly colored—pinks, blues, greens, and purples. But one dancer wore a slinky black dress with a long lace skirt. She had a bright red rose in her hair and a black lace fan in her hands. She was tapping her feet on the floor and practicing her spins. Katie thought she was beautiful.

"When is the show going to start?" Katie asked impatiently.

"Right away!" Annabelle leaped from her chair. She stomped her feet and clapped her hands high above her head. "Look at me!" she shouted. "I'm a flamenco dancer."

Katie laughed. Annabelle sure loved to dance.

"Come on, Katie," Annabelle urged.

This time, Katie didn't think twice. She jumped up and stomped her feet, just like she'd seen the woman in the black dress do.

Annabelle twirled around wildly. Katie whirled around, too. She turned and turned. Faster and faster. Until . . .

"Katie, watch where you're going!" Annabelle shouted.

The warning came too late. Katie fell backward—right into a waiter carrying a big tray filled with paella! Platters of rice, seafood, and sausage flew through the air.

A pile of rice landed on the head of a man who was sitting near the stage. A lobster claw fell onto his wife's head.

A big hunk of sausage hit another woman right in the eye.

A whole plate of paella flew toward stage . . . *and landed right on top of the dancer in the black dress*!

The dancer sat there for a moment, looking

down at her costume. She was covered with yellow rice. Shrimp, mussels, sausage, and clams peeked out from between the layers of black lace.

Katie hoped that the beautiful black dress wasn't ruined. "I'll get you some wet paper towels!" she called out to the dancer.

Quickly, Katie raced to the ladies' room. As the door slammed shut behind her, she grabbed some paper towels from the shelf and began to run them under the sink.

Suddenly, Katie felt a cool breeze blowing against her neck. She knew right away this was no ordinary breeze. "Oh, no!" Katie shouted out. "Not now!"

But there was no stopping the magic wind. The tornado grew so powerful, it knocked Katie to the ground.

And then it stopped. Just like that.

The magic wind was gone. Katie Carew was somebody new.

But who?

Chapter 15

Slowly, Katie opened her eyes and looked around. She wasn't in the bathroom anymore. Instead, she was standing on the stage. She glanced down. There, instead of her T-shirt and skirt, Katie saw a long black dress with a lace skirt. The dress was covered with greasy yellow rice and bits of seafood and sausage. The grease felt yucky on her skin.

She reached up to touch her hair. Her red pigtails were gone. Instead her hair was tied up in a bun. And there was a flower tucked behind one of her ears.

Oh, no! Katie had turned into the flamenco dancer!

The show would be starting soon. The audience would be expecting to see a real dancer. Katie wasn't a dancer at all. What was she going to do?

The music began to play. Quickly, Katie ran toward the backstage area. She had to get out of there before someone realized she wasn't really the dancer.

But it was too late. One of the male dancers took her by the arm. He wrapped his arm around her waist and began tap-dancing flamenco style. Before she knew it, Katie was out on stage.

Other dancers formed pairs behind Katie and her partner. They began tapping their feet and clapping their hands.

There was nothing Katie could do now. The show had to go on. She ran her hands up and down her skirt quickly, trying to wipe off at least some of the rice and the seafood. Then Katie began to stomp her feet to the beat.

At first, she seemed to be getting the rhythm.

"This isn't so hard," she said to herself. She stomped her feet harder.

"Ouch!" Katie's dance partner shouted in pain as she stepped on his foot.

"Sorry," Katie muttered. She waved her fan in front of her face and tried to twirl like she'd seen the real dancer do backstage.

The black lace fan whacked Katie's partner in the nose. He jumped backward, surprised.

"Oof!" one of the background dancers groaned as Katie's dance partner banged into her.

Katie raised her arms up in the air and clapped her hands while she stomped her feet. The other dancers stared and moved out of the way. They had no idea what she was doing.

But Katie kept going. She danced faster and faster, trying to make her way toward the backstage area. She was trying to get out of the spotlight as quickly as possible. If she could just get off the stage. Katie moved her legs faster, and faster, and . . .

BOOM!

Katie got off the stage, all right. She *fell* off—and landed right in the lap of a man sitting in the front row.

Katie's face turned bright red. She looked like such a fool! She was so embarrassed. This was the worst night ever!

Quickly, Katie leaped up and raced off toward the bathroom. It was the only place she could think of where she could get away from everyone.

Katie stood there, alone in the bathroom, staring at herself in the mirror. Black eye makeup was running down her cheeks. She sure didn't look like the beautiful, graceful dancer Katie had seen before.

She hadn't acted like a graceful dancer, either. In fact, she'd made a real mess of things. Everyone in the *tablao* had seen that. Even her parents and Annabelle.

105

For once, Katie was glad she was somebody else. If Annabelle had known that it was Katie up there, she never would have let her live that down.

Just then, Katie felt a cool breeze blowing on the back of her neck. The lace skirt began to rustle slightly.

Katie knew that this was no ordinary wind. This was the magic wind. The *magic* wind grew stronger and stronger. The fierce tornado circled Katie, blowing her skirt high in the air.

And then it stopped. Just like that.

The magic wind was gone. Katie Carew was back.

✕   ✕   ✕

"There you are!" Mrs. Carew called as Katie walked out of the bathroom and started to walk across the club. "I was getting worried about you. Where did you go?"

"I was in the bathroom," Katie told her.

"All this time?" Mrs. Carew asked.

Katie nodded. "It took a while to get the paella out of my hair. It was a mess."

"So was the show," Annabelle told her. She started giggling. "One of the dancers fell off the stage! You should have seen it. It was *so* funny!"

Katie frowned. "You shouldn't laugh," she told Annabelle. "It probably hurt a lot. And she was probably really embarrassed."

"She should be," Annabelle said.

"It's not so easy to dance in a flamenco show," Katie told her.

"Oh, come on," Annabelle argued. "How hard could it be?" She raised her arms in the air and began to stomp on the floor.

"Let's not start that again," Mr. Carew said as he steered the girls toward the exit. "I think we should get going."

As she left, Katie caught a glimpse of the dancer in the black dress. Her dress was torn, her fan had broken in two, and she seemed very confused. She had no idea how any of this had happened.

But Katie sure did. And she felt terrible about it.

Chapter 16

The next morning, Vicki took the tour group to the Plaza Mayor. The big square certainly looked different during the day than it had the night before. There were tour buses around. Katie could hear tour guides speaking to groups in all sorts of foreign languages.

Katie was happy that many of the little clubs hadn't opened yet. She certainly didn't want to run into anyone from the *tablao*.

As the tour group got off the bus, a short, round man came running over to Vicki. Katie recognized him right away. He was the manager of the flamenco club.

"Vicki, *un momento*," he said.

The tour guide turned around and smiled at him. Unfortunately, the club manager did not smile back. Instead, he began speaking very quickly in Spanish. He seemed very angry—especially when he glared at Katie and Annabelle.

Katie knew what that meant. She felt just awful. "Is something wrong?" she asked Vicki.

Vicki looked at her. "Carlos says there was a problem at his club last night. His lead dancer tripped over some food and ruined the dance. She's blaming you girls. And she's refusing to go onstage if children are allowed in the club."

"That's not fair!" Annabelle piped up. "It wasn't our fault that the dancer messed up."

Katie frowned. It really was her fault. And she knew it.

"People like to take their children to *tablaos*," Vicki told the girls. "So a lot of families canceled their reservations. And once word got out about the terrible show, other people canceled, too," Vicki explained. "The club will be empty tonight."

"That's not fair!" Katie exclaimed. "Flamenco dancing is very hard to do. It would be easy for someone to make a mistake."

"Oh, come on, Katie," Annabelle began.

"No. It's not as easy as it looks," Katie insisted. "Those dancers take flamenco lessons for years and . . ." She stopped suddenly and smiled brightly. "That's it!" she exclaimed.

"What's it?" Vicki asked.

"I know how Carlos can bring lots of customers to his club," Katie said. "He can have his dancers give flamenco lessons before the show."

Vicki thought for a moment. "I don't know of any club like that in Madrid," she said.

"That's what will make it so great. It will be a one-of-a-kind *tablao*!" Katie said excitedly. "And kids love to take dancing lessons. Maybe Carlos can convince his lead dancer to change her mind. I think she will. She seemed pretty nice to me."

"*Qué? Qué?*" Carlos asked.

"He's asking me what you're saying," Vicki told Katie. Then she began to talk to Carlos in Spanish.

Carlos was quiet for a moment, listening and thinking. Finally, he said something in Spanish and shrugged.

Vicki nodded and shook his hand.

"What did he say?" Katie asked Vicki nervously.

"He said it was worth a try," Vicki said. "I think so, too. In fact, tonight, we will all take a flamenco lesson. If it works out, I'll recommend the *tablao* to other tour guides."

"Oh, it will work out," Katie assured her. "It just has to."

Chapter 17

"Olé!" Katie's father shouted out as he stomped his feet.

Katie giggled. Her dad was not a very good dancer. But he sure was having a good time with his flamenco lesson. Everyone in the tour group was.

Annabelle was perched on her father's shoulders. She bounced up and down as he tapped his feet against the stage.

The Fishmans were dancing close. Mrs. Fishman waved a fan in front of her face. Mr. Fishman clapped his hands in the air.

The Penderbottoms were learning to use castanets. But they weren't very good at using them. The little instruments were clicking at all the wrong times.

Mrs. McIntyre danced by herself, while her husband took pictures of her with his video camera. The Garcias were busy taking pictures of each other with all of the professional dancers.

Miss Cornblau and Miss Framingham were giggling as a real flamenco dancer helped them to spin around and stomp their feet at the same time.

Vicki had asked some of her other tour-guide friends to bring their groups to the *tablao* for a flamenco lesson, so there were plenty of other tourists there, too. Some were speaking Japanese to one another. Some were speaking German. A few tourists were speaking Hebrew.

But Katie didn't have to speak their languages to know they were all having a good time. Their smiles and laughter told her that.

When the music stopped, Vicki leaped up onto the stage. "Okay, everyone, please take your seats," she said. "It's been a super night so far, hasn't it?"

Everyone cheered. It had been a fun time—yummy food and great dancing lessons.

"But the best is yet to come. It's time for the show," Vicki said.

As the lights went down, Annabelle turned to Mrs. Carew. "Where's Katie?" she asked.

"I don't know," Mrs. Carew said. "I thought she was with you."

"Maybe she went to the bathroom again," Annabelle suggested.

At that moment, the spotlight flashed toward the stage. The dancers took to the stage. All the performers from the night before were there—even the dancer in the black dress. But it was a new dancer who took center stage. She was dressed in a pink lacy dress that looked just beautiful with her bright red hair.

"It's Katie!" Annabelle squealed.

The dancer in the black skirt stepped up beside Katie. She tapped her feet three times. Katie tapped her feet three times. Then the dancer snapped her fingers in the air. Katie snapped *her* fingers, too. Then the dancer in the black dress spun around. Katie spun around, too—and this time she was careful not to go near the edge of the stage.

At the end of the dance, everyone applauded. The dancer in the black dress gave Katie a rose.

As she took her bow, Katie smiled at Carlos. Everyone was having a great time. His *tablao* was saved!

✕　✕　✕

"That was great fun!" Mrs. Penderbottom exclaimed as the dance show ended.

"I'm so glad we got the whole evening on videotape," Mrs. McIntyre added. "I can't wait to show everyone back home how I learned to do the flamenco."

"And I can't wait to tell the other tour directors about this *tablao*," Vicki said. "It's going to be a favorite stop for lots of people." She looked around. "Is everyone ready to leave?"

"In a minute," Katie piped up. "I have to change into my real clothes and give this dress back to Carlos." She frowned. "I sure hate to take off this beautiful costume."

As Katie began to walk away, Vicki whispered something to the club manager. Carlos whispered something back to her.

"Katie, wait," Vicki said. "You don't have to give the dress back. Carlos is giving it to you as a gift."

Katie was thrilled. She'd never owned anything as beautiful as this flamenco dress.

"I want a dress, too," Annabelle whined.

Vicki shook her head. "Sorry, Annabelle. It was Katie's great idea that saved Carlos's *tablao*. That's why he's giving it to her."

Annabelle pouted.

"Here, you can keep the fan," Katie told her. "Now we both have a souvenir from Madrid."

"Thanks, Katie!" Annabelle exclaimed. She gave Katie a big hug.

Carlos smiled. *"Katie es una buena amiga."*

"What does that mean?" Katie asked.

"He said you are a good friend," Vicki explained.

"She sure is," Annabelle said as she waved her new fan. "The best!"

Dear Louie,

I am writing to you from the Piazza San Marco in Venice, Italy. I just had a slice of pizza. It was cooked in a wood-burning oven and it had a very thin crust. It was good, but not as yummy as yours. Nothing beats your special sauce!

Arrivederci (that means good-bye).
Wish you were here,
Katie

Louie's Pizza Shop
Cherrydale
USA

Chapter 18

Katie stepped off the water bus and looked around at Venice. "Wow!" she exclaimed. "It's like a fairy-tale kingdom."

Vicki smiled. "A lot of people feel that way. The buildings are all so colorful, like gingerbread houses. And since there are no cars on the streets, the city feels really old-fashioned."

Katie nodded. It was kind of weird not to see any buses or cars, like there had been in the other cities they'd visited.

But you couldn't drive in Venice even if you had a car. There were too many water canals. Venice was really a group of islands connected by stone bridges. The bridges made it possible to walk from one part of the city to the next.

"I like going everywhere by boat," Katie said. "It's fun."

"Being on the water makes me hungry," Annabelle remarked.

Katie giggled. "Everything makes you hungry," she teased.

Annabelle pointed to a small white stand just outside the hotel. There were pictures of ice-cream cones on a sign nearby. "Those look yummy," she said.

"Oh, so you want a gelato," Vicki said.

"No, I want ice cream," Annabelle corrected her.

"It's called gelato here," Vicki explained. "You'll love it. Italian ice cream is amazing!"

Annabelle's dad handed the girls a few coins. "Go ahead and get some," he told them.

The girls smiled excitedly and ran over to the ice-cream stand. Katie didn't speak any Italian, so she pointed to a picture of a strawberry cone.

"You like strawberry?" the teenager
behind the stand asked her in broken English.

"You speak English?" Katie replied,
surprised.

"I try to practice English," he told her. "Is hard for me. But important."

"You speak very well," Katie told him.

"Well, it wasn't perfect . . ." Annabelle began.

"It was great," Katie interrupted her.

"Thank you," the ice-cream salesman said. He held out his hand. "My name is Vincenzo."

"I'm Katie. And this is Annabelle."

"Pleased to meet you," Vincenzo replied.

"Do you make this ice cream?" Katie asked him.

Vincenzo shook his head. "No. I just sell it for a man in my neighborhood. This is not what I want to do forever. I really want to be a gondolier, like my father."

"*A what?*" Katie asked.

Vincenzo pointed to a long, wooden canoe-like boat. It was docked between two red-and-white striped poles. An older man was standing in the back of the boat. He was wearing a red-and-white striped shirt.

"That is our gondola," Vincenzo explained. "My father takes tourists around Venice in it. He sings to them. A man who steers a gondola boat is called a gondolier."

"So he just floats around Venice all day?" Annabelle asked. "That sounds like fun."

"Is hard work," Vincenzo told her. "I know."

"Have you steered a gondola before?" Katie asked him.

Vincenzo shook his head sadly. "My father will not let me take the gondola out with customers. But I would be a great gondolier."

Vincenzo looked very sad.

"Why won't your father let you steer the gondola?" Katie asked him.

"He says I am too young," Vincenzo explained. "But I am not. I am almost eighteen. And I am strong enough to paddle a big gondola."

"So you *have* done it before?" Katie asked, confused.

"Oh, yes!" Vincenzo said proudly. "I practice early in the morning, before anyone is awake. But I do not tell my father."

"Maybe you *should* tell him," Katie said. "He might be proud that you are working so hard."

"He would not like it," Vincenzo insisted as he handed her a strawberry gelato.

"You'll have to tell him sometime. Especially if you want a chance to be a gondolier," Katie reminded him.

"I do not think he will ever let me try," Vincenzo said. "He does not trust anyone but himself with the gondola. I wish he could see how good I am."

Suddenly Katie began to get one of her great ideas. "Maybe you could ask him if you could take one trip, you know, sort of like a test. And if it goes really well . . ."

"I am not sure my father would like that," Vincenzo said. "And I do not think too many tourists would want to be with a gondolier on his first trip. They usually like to be with gondoliers who have been doing this a long time."

"Everyone has to have a first time," Katie said. "I would go with you."

"So would I," Annabelle agreed, taking a big bite of her gelato. "And I could get my parents to go, too."

But Vincenzo wasn't sure about all this. "My father wants me to wait . . ." he began.

"Just ask him," Katie interrupted him. "What do you have to lose? If he says no, you can still sell gelato here at the hotel."

Vincenzo thought for a moment and then nodded. "Okay. I will do it. It is worth the try."

Chapter 19

"Come on, Katie, hurry up," Mrs. Carew called out as she walked out of the hotel the following morning. "We have a lot of shopping to do."

But Katie did not hurry. She didn't want to go shopping. It seemed like that's all her mother had done since they'd arrived in Venice.

"Now remember, don't touch anything," her mom continued. "If you break it, we'll have to buy it. Venetian glass is very expensive."

"Come on, kiddo, perk up. We're going to have fun," Mr. Carew added.

Katie scowled. *Fun? Yeah, right.*

Just then, Annabelle walked out the door with her family. "What are you doing today?" she asked Katie.

"Shopping," Katie groaned. "For water glasses."

"Gosh, I'm sorry," Annabelle said.

Before Katie could ask Annabelle what she and her family had planned, she heard someone calling her name.

"Katie! Katie!"

Katie turned around and smiled. It was Vincenzo. He was hurrying toward her.

"Buongiorno," he said, using the Italian word for good morning.

"Good morning," Katie answered.

"I have to thank you," Vincenzo told her.

"For what?" Katie asked.

"For convincing me to ask my father to give me a test with our gondola," Vincenzo explained. "He has agreed. I take my first boat out today!"

"Oh, wow!" Katie cheered.

"Of course, I want you to be on that boat," Vincenzo told her. "You will be my guest."

"Mom! Dad! Can we go? Please?" Katie pleaded.

Mrs. Carew shook her head. "I'm sorry, Katie. We already made plans to shop today. I hired a water taxi to take us around to the stores. We'll go on a gondola ride tomorrow."

Katie didn't want to shop all day. She wanted to take *this* gondola ride. With Vincenzo.

"We can go, can't we?" Annabelle asked her parents.

Mrs. Bridgeman shrugged. "I guess we can. We did want to take a gondola ride at some point." She turned to Mrs. Carew. "We'll take Katie if you'd like."

Katie looked up at her parents hopefully.

Mrs. Carew laughed. "Oh, dear. I can't refuse that face. Okay, you can go."

"Wonderful!" Vincenzo cheered. "The

gondola ride will begin at one o'clock. I will see you there!"

$$\times \quad \times \quad \times$$

Sure enough, at one o'clock, Vincenzo was standing right near his gondola at the dock near the hotel. He looked very professional in his red-and-white striped shirt and big hat.

"*Buongiorno,*" he greeted Katie and the Bridgemans. "It is very nice to see you."

"*Buongiorno,*" Katie replied.

Katie squinted into the bright sunlight. She could barely see. "Do I have time to run back to my hotel room and get my sunglasses?" she asked Vincenzo.

"Of course, Katie," Vincenzo answered.

Katie turned and ran back to the hotel. She hurried into the elevator and pushed the button for her floor.

As the elevator door shut, Katie felt a cool breeze blowing on the back of her neck. She looked around for an air conditioning vent. But she couldn't find one. There were no windows, either. In fact, there was no way for wind to be blowing in the elevator . . . at least not a normal wind.

The magic wind, on the other hand, could blow anywhere!

And, boy, was it blowing! Katie shut her eyes and tried not to cry as the tornado raged.

Katie really didn't want to switcheroo into someone else. Especially not when she was about to go on her first gondola ride. But the magic wind didn't care what Katie wanted.

Suddenly, the tornado stopped blowing. Just like that.

The magic wind was gone. And so was Katie.

Chapter 20

Katie opened her eyes slowly and looked around. She was outside the hotel near the water. There were gondolas all around.

"Vincenzo, will you help me into the boat?" Mrs. Bridgeman asked. "I'm not very steady on my feet."

Vincenzo? Katie looked around, hoping her friend was standing behind her. But no luck. Mrs. Bridgeman was staring right at Katie.

That was because Katie had turned into Vincenzo! She was wearing his red-and-white striped shirt and his big hat. Katie was going to have to take Vincenzo's gondola test for him. And she knew *nothing* about gondolas!

What was she going to do?

At first, Katie thought about canceling the ride. But she couldn't do that. Vincenzo's father would never let him take the gondola out after that.

This whole test had been Katie's idea. She would have to steer the boat. Otherwise she would ruin everything.

"Of course I'll help you," Katie said as she took Mrs. Bridgeman's hand and led her into the boat. Annabelle and her father followed close behind.

Katie stood there in the back of the boat for a moment, watching as the other gondoliers steered their boats down the canal. It didn't look very hard. If Katie could just follow them, she'd be fine.

BONG!

Just then, the bell from the big church in the square rang out. It was one o'clock. The gondola cruise was supposed to start.

"I hope Katie gets here soon," Mrs.

Bridgeman said. "We have reservations for lunch at three o'clock. We need to be back in time to change."

Katie gulped. She knew Katie wasn't coming back. At least not for a while.

"We'll go without her," she told Mrs. Bridgeman. "A tour with three people is as nice as a tour with four people."

"But we can't leave a little girl alone in Venice," Annabelle's mother said.

"She isn't alone," Katie said. "I saw your tour guide Vicki in your hotel lobby. She can take care of Katie for the day."

"I don't know . . ." Mrs. Bridgeman began.

But Katie didn't wait for her to finish her thought. With one hard push of her gondolier's pole, she forced the boat down the canal. They were off!

"Hey, aren't gondoliers supposed to sing while they work?" Annabelle asked after they had been traveling a while.

"Yes, let's hear a nice Italian song," Mr. Bridgeman urged.

Uh-oh! Katie didn't know how to sing anything in Italian. In fact the only song she knew that was even *about* something Italian was something she'd learned in kindergarten.

That was going to have to do.

"On top of spaghetti, all covered with cheese," she began to sing. "I lost my poor meatball when somebody sneezed."

"Oh. I know that one!" Annabelle shouted. She began to sing along. "It rolled off the table, and under a bush . . ."

Soon the Bridgemans joined in as well. And they kept on singing the song all the way down the big canal.

Katie began to relax. Annabelle and her parents were having a good time. Everything was going to be all right.

After a while, though, Katie grew tired. Steering a gondola was not as easy as it looked. Even with Vincenzo's strong arms to help her, Katie was really achy. It was getting harder and harder to move the big pole through the water.

"Why aren't we going any faster?" Annabelle asked. "All the other gondolas are way ahead."

"It's not a race, honey," her father told her.

"Exactly," Katie said. "I'm giving you a chance to get a good look at our beautiful city."

Annabelle seemed happy with that answer. Which was a good thing, since Katie wasn't paddling anymore. Her arms were too tired. The gondola was floating all on its own.

The Bridgemans seemed to enjoy floating through Venice, though. They were staring at the beautiful houses that lined the narrow canal. The brick and cement houses were painted pretty colors like pink, red, and yellow. There were balconies outside the windows, most of which had been decorated

with beautiful flowers.

Katie thought Venice was the most magical city she'd even seen. For a little while, she forgot she was supposed to be Vincenzo. She felt like any other tourist looking at the city, floating like the people in the other gondolas.

Katie glanced ahead at the other boats . . .

UH-OH! The other gondolas were gone!

Katie gulped. They must have continued down the big canal. But Katie's gondola wasn't in the big canal anymore. Somehow they'd drifted into a tiny little canal. Now Katie had no idea where they were.

Even worse, she had no idea how to get back.

Chapter 21

"Vincenzo, don't you think we should be turning back now?" Mr. Bridgeman asked a few moments later. "It's already been more than an hour."

Katie nodded. She wanted to turn back. More than anything. She just didn't know how.

"I . . . um . . ." she started, feeling very sad and frightened. This was going so wrong. Not only was she lost in Venice, but she was going to ruin everything for Vincenzo. When his father found out that the gondola had gotten lost . . .

Katie shook her head. She didn't want to

think about it.

Instead, she forced herself to think of a way she could fix this mess. She had been lost before, with her parents. There was that time they'd driven to the Grand Canyon. Her father had refused to stop and ask for directions. But her mother had insisted. So they'd stopped at a coffee shop to ask for help. While her mother found out how to get to the highway, Katie had ordered a milkshake. They'd gotten to the Grand Canyon just fine.

That was it! Katie would stop somewhere and ask for directions back to the hotel.

But it wasn't that easy here. She was in Italy, not America. And Katie didn't speak Italian. She could never understand the directions.

Tears began to form in Katie's eyes. They were never getting back to the hotel. They would be floating around Venice forever and ever. She would never see Pepper or her parents again!

Just then, the gondola floated by a small pastry shop. A sign in the window caught Katie's eye. It said:

English spoken here.

Phew! Talk about luck.

"We'll go back to the hotel," Katie assured the Bridgemans. "But first, we'll stop for delicious Italian pastry. Venice is famous for its sweets!"

Quickly, she steered the gondola up to dock outside the shop.

× × ×

As Annabelle and her parents ate their sweet, creamy cakes, Katie went to speak to the owner of the pastry shop. At first, the woman behind the counter didn't believe Katie's story.

"What do you mean, you're a gondolier and you're lost?" she asked. "Gondoliers know this city better than anyone."

"I'm not really a gondolier," Katie whispered.

×

The woman looked at Katie's red-and-white striped shirt. "You're not?" she asked.

"Well, I . . . um . . . the thing is . . . it's my first trip," Katie stammered. "My father is giving me a test. I'm not doing very well."

The woman nodded. "I understand that. The first time my father let me make the cream puffs, I left the cream out too long. Cream puffs don't taste very good when the cream is spoiled." She smiled kindly at Katie. "I'll help you."

Katie gave the woman the name and address of her hotel. The woman drew her a map, showing which canals would lead her back home.

"Thank you," Katie told her.

"You're welcome," the woman replied. "You're going to be a very good gondolier someday. Your English is perfect. You sound almost like an American."

Katie grinned. If she only knew.

After the gondola pushed off from the pastry shop, Katie followed the map. She pushed the big boat around turns and curves, moving through several small canals, before reaching the wide Grand Canal.

Several other gondolas came into view. They would be back at the hotel soon. Happily, Katie began to hum a familiar song under her breath.

"I know that one!" Annabelle shouted out. "That's by the Bayside Boys. How do you know about them?"

Oops. Katie had forgotten she was supposed to be an Italian teenager instead of an American fourth-grader. "Um, we have a lot of American music here," she said quickly. "The tourists bring their CDs."

"Hey, your English is getting pretty good," Annabelle remarked. "You sounded almost like one of us that time."

Oops.

"Do you know this song?" Annabelle

continued. She began to sing another Bayside Boys tune.

Katie and Annabelle kept on singing all the way back to the hotel. When they reached the dock, Katie pulled the boat between two of the red-and-white striped poles. Then she expertly hopped out and helped Mr. and Mrs. Bridgeman to shore. Annabelle climbed out by herself.

Katie smiled broadly. She'd brought everyone back safe and sound. Everything had turned out just fine.

Or . . . *maybe* not! At that moment, Vincenzo's father came running over. He began screaming in Italian. As he yelled, he pointed to a group of people standing nearby. They were obviously waiting for their gondola ride. Katie had been very late bringing back the boat.

Mr. and Mrs. Bridgeman weren't very happy either. "Oh, no. Look at the time. We missed our reservation in the restaurant," Mr.

Bridgeman said angrily. "This was only supposed to be a one-hour ride. It's been over two hours."

Katie wanted to cry. But she figured the real Vincenzo wouldn't do that. So she just stood there, listening to everyone screaming at her. It was awful. But eventually, Vincenzo's father went off to give his customers their ride. And the Bridgemans went back into the hotel.

Katie was alone. She was also tired and hungry. She walked over to Vincenzo's gelato stand. No one was around, because the stand was closed. Katie crouched down behind the stand and sat down. It was the perfect place to hide. No one could find her there.

Well maybe no *person* could find her. But something else did. All of a sudden, Katie felt a familiar breeze blowing around her. She knew immediately that the magic wind was back.

Katie wasn't entirely sorry to have the

wind come back. It had caused a real mess this time. She was anxious to become Katie Carew again.

And then the wind stopped. Just like that. Katie Carew was as good as new! Well, *almost* as good as new. She still felt pretty awful about what she'd done to Vincenzo.

Chapter 22

All the next day, Katie tried hard to avoid
Vincenzo. She didn't know what to say to him.
She wished she could apologize. But how
could she explain what the magic wind had
done? It was just easier to stay away.

But that night, as she and Annabelle
walked out of the hotel with their parents
and Vicki, she bumped right into him. He was
unloading ice cream into his freezer. He
looked very sad.

"Hi, Vincenzo," Katie said quietly.

"Hello, Katie," he replied sadly. "Have you
heard about what happened?"

Katie nodded. "I'm sorry."

Vincenzo shrugged. "It is strange. I do not understand it. One minute I am near the boat ready to go, and the next . . . well, I am not sure what happened. All I know is I ruined everything."

"Ruined?" Annabelle piped up. "Are you crazy? That was the best gondola ride ever!"

Vicki and the Bridgemans looked at her strangely.

"The best?" Vicki asked. "I thought it went on too long, and you wound up stopping for pastry on some little canal instead of coming straight back to the hotel."

Annabelle nodded. "We did. And we sang Bayside Boys songs."

"We did?" Vincenzo asked.

"Sure," Annabelle said. "Don't you remember?"

"I guess so. I mean no. I mean . . ." Vincenzo sighed. "I do not know . . ."

"It was the first fun thing I've done since we got to Venice," Annabelle continued. "It wasn't a museum or a fancy restaurant or some old church. It was the perfect ride for a kid!"

"I wish you could tell my father that," Vincenzo moaned.

Katie looked over toward the canal, where Vincenzo's father was busy cleaning the gondola. "Why can't she?" she asked.

"Huh?" Vincenzo and Annabelle asked together.

"Annabelle should tell your father about all the fun she had," Katie said excitedly. "It would be a great activity for kids to go on while their parents shop for crystal or go to a fancy restaurant."

"You know, that's not a bad idea," Vicki said. "I'm always looking for things kids can do in Europe. And I know parents like some time alone on vacation."

"That's true," Mr. Carew agreed. "Katie would definitely have hated going shopping today."

"Do you really think my father would like this idea?" Vincenzo asked.

Katie smiled. "We won't know until we ask him!"

The very next morning, Katie happily took a seat on Vincenzo's very first official Kids' Cruise. She was so excited . . . especially when Vincenzo handed each kid on the cruise a yummy gelato.

There were five kids on the gondola. With a hard push of his pole, Vincenzo steered the gondola down the canal. As they traveled past the colorful houses, Annabelle shouted out, "Vincenzo, will you sing 'On Top of Spaghetti' again?"

Vincenzo looked at her. "I do not know that song," he said.

"Sure, you do," Annabelle told him. "We sang it yesterday, remember?"

Uh-oh. Katie knew Vincenzo wasn't going to remember that. But she sure did. "I'll sing

it with you, Annabelle," Katie said, quickly. "On top of spaghetti, all covered with cheese . . ."

"I lost my poor meatball when somebody sneezed," Annabelle added. Before long, all the kids had joined in.

Katie smiled as they cruised down the canal. This time the trip was going really well. Vincenzo was going to be a gondolier!

The magic wind hadn't ruined his career after all. So there!

Chapter 23

The next evening, Katie and Annabelle sat beside each other in the back room of a restaurant near Venice's Grand Canal. Katie giggled as Annabelle placed three strands of spaghetti in her mouth and quickly slurped them up.

"Good one." Katie laughed. She was having a great time. Too bad it was all about to end. This was her last night in Europe. The people in her tour group were having one final meal together.

The Garcias and the McIntyres were passing around some pictures they'd taken during the trip.

"Oh, look," Mrs. Garcia said. "That's me being a gargoyle at Notre Dame!"

"And here we are at Buckingham Palace," Mrs. McIntyre said. "We were pretending to be guards, remember?"

Katie frowned. She'd been a guard there, too. Only she hadn't been pretending.

"Here's Katie and Annabelle acting like penguins at Faunia," Mr. McIntyre said as he pulled another photo from the pile.

"That was a fun day," Annabelle exclaimed. "Wasn't it, Katie?"

Katie nodded. They had all been fun days. She looked around the table. The grown-ups were exchanging addresses and phone numbers so they could stay in touch. Even the adults didn't want to say good-bye.

But they had to. It was time to go home.

"Good-bye, Europe," Katie whispered quietly to herself. *"Au revoir, adiós, arrivederci."*

Dear Annabelle,

This is a picture of Pepper in front of our house. I hope you like your new house in Houston. Maybe on my next vacation I can visit you.

Wish you were here!

Katie

Annabelle Bridgeman
Houston
USA